ÆSOP'S FABLES

ILLUSTRATED BY FULVIO TESTA

ÆSOP'S FABLES

ILLUSTRATED BY FULVIO TESTA

BARRON'S

New York • London • Toronto • Sydney

English translation © Copyright 1989 by Barron's Educational Series. Inc.
© Copyright 1989 by Edizioni Scolastiche Walk Over, Bergamo, Italy
© Copyright 1989 by Fulvio Testa

The title of the Italian edition is "Favole di Esopo"

All inquiries should be addressed to:
Barron's Educational Series, Inc.
250 Wireless Boulevard
Hauppauge, NY 11788

Library of Congress Catalog Card No. 88-24126

International Standard Book No. 0-8120-5958-1

Library of Congress Cataloging-in-Publication Data
Aesop's fables.
    Aesop's fables/illustrated by Fulvio Testa.
    p.cm..
    Summary: An illustrated collection of twenty traditional fables including "The Hares And The Frogs." "The Cat And The Mouse," and "The Wolf And The Heron."
    ISBN 0-8120-5958-1
    1. Fables. [1. Fables.] I. Testa, Fulvio, ill. II. Title. PZ8.2.A254 1989
398.2'452—dc19   88-24126
                                                                      CIP
                                                                       AC

Printed in Italy
901 987654321

TABLE OF CONTENTS

THE OLD LION AND THE FOX

An old lion, too weak to catch his prey by force, thought he could get his food by being clever.

So he set himself up in a cave and lay down, pretending to be sick.

Every time an animal came to visit him, the lion seized it and ate it up.

He had already captured many animals when a clever fox came along and figured out this trick.

The fox came near the cave but kept a certain distance away and asked about the lion's health.

"Oh, it's really quite bad," complained the lion. "But, please, why don't you come in?"

"I would come in with great pleasure," replied the fox, "if I hadn't seen so many animal footprints that go into your cave but don't come out!"

THE FOX
AND THE STORK

One day the fox invited the stork to dinner.

They sat down at the table but, alas, the stork was served a clear broth in a large bowl.

All her efforts were in vain. There was no way to sip even a drop from that bowl with her long beak.

When it was the stork's turn to invite the fox to dinner, she prepared a tasty little meal with a great deal of care.

But, alas, the fox was served many little pieces of food placed at the bottom of a jar with a long, narrow neck.

The stork could eat easily by putting her long beak into the jar, but the fox could only watch hungrily. Not even the tip of his nose could fit into the long, narrow jar.

"You see, I followed your example," said the stork to the fox. Then, with great relish, she devoured the very last bite.

THE WOLF
AND HIS SHADOW

A wolf was walking along a plain at dusk. As he walked, he admired his shadow, which kept getting longer and longer.

"Someone like me would certainly never be afraid of a lion! Just look! I am longer than a house!"

And, full of pride, he added, "Soon I will be the king of all the animals!"

But at that very moment, the lion arrived and, not at all frightened by the huge shadow, swallowed the wolf in one mouthful.

THE WOLF AND THE HERON

A wolf had swallowed a big bone and it stuck in his throat.

He went everywhere hoping to find someone who could get it out.

Finally, he met a heron and begged her to pull the bone out of his throat.

In exchange he promised her a great reward.

The heron stuck her beak and then her whole head into the throat of the wolf and pulled out the bone.

"I've done it! Now give me what you have promised," the heron said.

"My friend, after putting your head into the mouth of a wolf, you should be happy to have it back in one piece!" replied the wolf. "What more could you ask for?"

THE LION AND THE BOAR

One dry, sunny summer day a lion and a boar went to drink at the same pool of water.

They soon began to argue over who should drink first, and they ended up challenging each other to a duel.

The battle scene became quite frantic with each animal receiving dreadful bites and blows from the other.

All worn out, they finally stopped to catch their breath. While resting, the lion and the boar saw some vultures nearby who were watching them carefully. The vultures' mouths were watering as they wondered which of the two would end up a corpse on the ground.

At this point the two duelists looked at each other and decided to stop their bloody battle.

"It would be better to remain friends," they said to each other, "than to become tasty morsels for vultures."

THE LION, THE HARE, AND THE DEER

A lion was about to devour a hare that was sleeping at the edge of a field, when he saw a deer passing by.

The lion left the hare to his nap. A moment later, the hare awoke and, quicker than a wink, ran far, far away.

In the meantime the lion began to chase the deer, but, as fast as he ran, he could not catch it.

Exhausted, he went back to look for the hare. When the lion reached the edge of the field, he discovered that the hare had run away.

"Let this be a lesson for me," he told himself. "While trying to get something better, I lost what I already had within my grasp."

THE FOX
AND THE GRAPES

A hungry fox went all around the countryside, but could not find anything to fill his empty stomach.

Finally, the beautiful color of grapes ripening in the sun caught his attention.

Standing under the vine he stared up at the big juicy bunch of grapes and thought he had finally solved his problem.

He tried to grasp them by reaching up with his paws.

He jumped and jumped and jumped…but he could not get them.

"Just a bunch of sour grapes! Who wants them anyway?" he said to himself as he walked away.

THE FOX AND THE CROW

A crow who had stolen a piece of meat was sitting high up on the branch of a tree.

A fox came by and saw him and his wonderful piece of red meat. So he went under the tree and said, "Crow, you are beautiful! You have feathers that are black as night and shiny as wet leaves! And what a tail you have! A real flower from the sky. And your wings? It is said that the eagle's are beautiful, but they haven't seen yours! And you fly terrifically, my dear crow! You could be king of the birds…or better still, of all the animals…if only you had…"

And the fox was silent.

The crow, up above, tilted his head and looked down impatiently. He would have liked to ask what it was that he didn't have, but because he had the meat in his beak, he couldn't say a word.

The fox sighed and finally said, "If only you had a *voice,* my dear!"

The crow fidgeted on the branch. Down below, the fox was quietly sighing and smoothing the grass with his big tail.

And so the crow opened his beak and yelled, "Caw! Caw! Caw! Who says I don't have a voice? Caw! Caw! Caw!"

The fox didn't stay around to listen. He grabbed the meat the crow let fall and ran away screaming, "You have a voice, my dear crow. But you need something else to become king of the animals. A brain!"

THE LION
AND THE MOUSE

Once there was a sleeping lion. A mouse came along and, thinking the lion was a mountain, ran up and down his body. But the lion, who felt something tickling him, woke up. With a quick move of his paw, he caught the mouse.

"Now, I'm going to eat you," he said.

"Why?" said the mouse. "I am so little that you would still be hungry. And just think—if you don't eat me, one day you might need my help!"

"I, need *your* help?" laughed the lion. "Ah, mouse, you are really very funny. For this I will spare you."

And so the lion let the mouse go free and forgot all about him.

A little while later, some hunters caught the lion and tied him up with strong rope. Then they went away to get help. The lion roared, pulled, and ripped at the rope, but it didn't break. Finally, the lion threw himself on the ground without any hope of saving himself.

Then he felt something tickling him. Suddenly, the mouse jumped up right in front of his nose.

"What a nice rope to chew!" said the mouse. "Thank goodness I am a live mouse and can help my friend!"

Without waiting, the mouse began to gnaw with his sharp teeth. In no time, the rope broke and the lion was freed.

"Blessed is the day I did not eat you!" said the lion as he ran away, while the mouse hopped about in his mane, laughing merrily.

THE HARES
AND THE FROGS

One day the hares got together to complain that their lives were so uncertain and full of fear. Everyone wanted them for their prey—men, dogs, eagles, and many other animals.

"It's better to get it over with than to live in constant fear and anxiety," they said.

Once they had made their decision, they all rushed toward the pond to dive in and drown.

Some frogs who were crouched around the pond heard this thunderous noise. Terrified, they all jumped into the water.

At the sight of this, one of the hares who was more sensible than the others said, "Stop! Everybody! Don't make this terrible mistake! Now you have seen that, so far as fear is concerned, there are animals that are even worse off than we are!"

THE TORTOISE AND THE HARE

The hare always made fun of the tortoise.

"How slow you are! How slow you are! Look at me: with only one jump I can go farther than you can with ten steps!"

And he went on and on.

One day the tortoise said to the hare, "The fastest one doesn't always arrive first."

"What?" laughed the hare. "Are you trying to say if we have a race you would finish first?"

"I am only saying what I said," replied the tortoise. "Let's have a race and we will see what happens."

And so they started. In an instant, the hare was a long way off. But he stopped and thought, "What pleasure is there in winning so quickly? I'm going to stop and wait for the tortoise. That way I will enjoy my victory more!"

The hare sat down under a bush and waited for the tortoise to arrive. He waited and waited. Finally, he became very sleepy, closed his eyes, and fell asleep.

While the hare was sleeping, the tortoise went slowly by. When he saw the hare, he went even more slowly so he wouldn't wake him up. And so the tortoise continued on his way.

After a little while the wind rustled the bush and the hare woke up. He remembered the race, got up, and ran as fast as he could toward the finish line. But the tortoise had arrived there before he did.

"You are much faster than I," said the tortoise to the hare, "but as you have seen, slow and steady wins the race!"

THE FROG AND THE OX

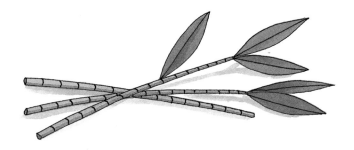

A frog saw a big, strong ox near the pond.

"If only I were like that," he thought.

"Listen to him," commented a friend from among the reeds. "All he can do is dream about being bigger than he is."

The frog was so small that the ox did not see him. But the frog, who could see the ox very well, was so amazed by his size that he almost died of envy.

And so he puffed himself up as big as he could and asked the other frogs if he was now bigger than the ox.

"Not yet," they answered.

The frog puffed up again and asked once more, "Who...who is bigger now?"

"The ox," answered the frogs.

Indignant, the frog tried again and puffed himself up still more. This time he puffed himself up so much that he actually split his skin.

"You see," remarked one of the other frogs, "there's no way you can make yourself any bigger than you actually are."

THE DOG
AND THE SHELL

A dog who loved to eat eggs saw a big pile of white shells in a basket.

"I'm really going to have a bellyful today!" he thought, mistaking them for eggs.

Then he opened his mouth up wide and swallowed the biggest one whole.

After a little while he began to feel a heavy weight in his stomach and a great deal of pain.

"This serves me right," he howled, now that he understood his mistake.

"How did I ever get it into my silly head that everything that's round is an egg?"

THE CICADA AND THE ANTS

The cicada was happy and content as he sat and sang on a leaf.

He could not understand why the ants worked so hard, even in summer.

"Carrying grain in this heat! How crazy!"

Time passed and winter arrived. One day the hungry cicada came to the ants while they were drying their grain in the sun.

"Will you give me some of your grain? You have so much!"

"But why didn't you put some away last summer?" they replied.

"I didn't have time," answered the cicada. "I had to sing."

"If you sang in the summer, then you can dance in the winter!" said the ants, laughing.

THE BOAR
AND THE FOX

A boar was standing next to a tree sharpening his tusks on the trunk.

A fox went by and looked at him.

He was working so hard that the tree and the nearby shrubs were all shaking.

"You are sharpening your tusks," said the fox, "but there is no sign of a hunter nor anyone who threatens you. Why are you troubling yourself?"

"The answer is obvious," replied the boar. "If something were to attack me, I certainly would not have the time to sharpen my tusks. But if I have them ready, I'll be able to put them to good use!"

THE LITTLE BIRD AND THE BAT

A little bird sat in a cage near a window. As night fell she started to sing her song.

A bat saw her and heard her singing. He came up and asked why she never sang during the day, but only in the dark.

"I have my reasons," replied the little bird. "You see, it was while I was singing during the day that I was captured and put in this cage. This was a lesson I will never forget!"

"But it doesn't do any good to be careful now," said the bat. "You should have done it *before* they caught you!"

THE CAT
AND THE MOUSE

There were many mice living in a house. A cat discovered this, went to live there, and began to eat them—one by one.

Finally, after many of them had been eaten, the mice decided to hide in their holes where the cat could not reach them.

Since the cat could not catch them, he decided to make them come out again by being clever.

So he climbed up a wall, hung himself on a coatrack, and pretended to be dead.

One of the mice, who was peeking out of his hole, said, "It's no use, my friend. I would stay far away from you even if you turned yourself into an empty bag."

THE WOLF
AND THE GOAT

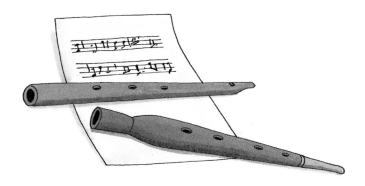

A goat strayed behind the rest of his flock. He was all alone and suddenly he realized a wolf was following him. He turned around and said, "I know you are thinking about eating me up in one, big gulp. But, please, if I have to die, let me at least have one last wish. Could you just play the flute so I can dance a little?"

While the wolf was playing and the goat was dancing, some dogs heard the music and came running after the wolf.

The wolf, running as fast as he could to escape, looked back for a moment to say to the goat.

"It serves me right! That will teach me to be a musician when it's my job to be a butcher!"

THE DONKEY
AND THE DOG

A donkey and a dog were traveling along together when they saw a letter on the ground.

The donkey picked it up, opened the envelope, and began to read the letter to the dog.

The letter concerned hay, barley and bran. But, since the dog was not interested in hay, barley or bran, he became very bored. Finally, he interrupted his friend.

"Please go on a little more. Maybe if you skipped a few lines you might find some information about meat and bones."

The donkey looked through the whole letter but didn't find anything about that kind of food.

"Throw it away, then," said the dog impatiently. "It's worthless stuff!"

But the donkey, who loved to eat hay, barley and bran, found the letter fascinating. "Wait a bit," he said, and he read the letter through to the very end.

THE BABY CRAB
AND HER MOTHER

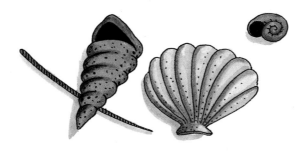

The mother crab spoke to her daughter.

"Be careful, my child, not to walk so crookedly on the sand. And don't always rub your side against the wet rock."

"All right, Mama," the baby crab answered. "But if you want me to follow your example, then *you* must walk straight, too. I will do whatever you do."

Aesop is the name traditionally given by the ancient Greeks to the author of their famous collection of animal fables. It is not known for certain if Aesop existed as a historical personage, or if instead, he is as much a legend as the stories attributed to him. The first known written collection of Aesop's fables was produced in the 4th century B.C.